The Treasure Ship of St Isabella

Written by Frank Pedersen
Illustrated by Paul Könye

Contents

For learning solutions, visit **cengage.com.au**

Meet the Characters

Jennifer

An 11-year-old girl.

Peter

Jennifer's father, a geologist and diver.

Miguel

The captain of Peter's exploration vessel.

Dear Reader

Over 100 Spanish ships sank in the Caribbean Sea between 1500 and 1750, many of them carrying gold, silver and precious jewels from South America. Storms, pirates and attacks from other ships caused most of the losses. What's interesting is that fewer than 50 of those shipwrecks have been found. Here's a story about one of the "lost" ships!

Frank Pedersen

Author

The Caribbean Sea

1. Cuba
2. Jamaica
3. St Isabella
4. San Antero
5. Caracas

1 A Caribbean Paradise

Jennifer watched the fiery Caribbean sunset fill the sky. The sand into which she buried her bare feet was still warm from the sun that had just slipped below a shimmering golden horizon.

A few metres along the beach, her father Peter was scooping sand out of a shallow pit. Twenty minutes earlier, a driftwood fire had been glowing in the pit. Peter had covered the embers with a layer of sand, dinner, and more sand.

"Are you ready for the main course?" he grinned. He took two parcels wrapped in steaming newspaper from the pit.

"Absolutely," smiled Jennifer, who was suddenly hungry. Peter and Jennifer both unwrapped their parcels. Stuck to the newspaper, the skin of the whole fish that lay within peeled off to reveal a feast of steaming, freshly cooked flesh.

"Who needs an oven, when you have a beach to cook in?" winked Jennifer's father.

"Or a table with knives and forks?" added Jennifer, popping a flake of juicy fish into her mouth.

Peter looked at the sunset sweeping across the sky and smiled. "This is better than the fish fingers I used to cook back in the city," he said.

"Back home, there weren't any reefs to go diving on, Dad," said Jennifer.

"That's true," agreed her father. "And the dive tanks I practised in never seemed to have any fresh fish swimming in them either!"

The pair laughed. Since Peter had got a job with the oil company, mapping the seabed around the Caribbean island of St Isabella, life had certainly changed.

Jennifer found it hard to imagine her previous life. A month ago, she was watching the traffic inching its way through the crowded streets below their tenth-floor apartment.

Now, the only things inching past were sand crabs or the sail of a distant yacht, far out to sea.

St Isabella lay at the end of a string of islands curving out into the Caribbean Sea. Largely ignored by tourists and cruise ships intent on visiting more well-known destinations, the island had been chosen as a base for Peter's seabed mapping because it was close to the oil-rich nation of Venezuela. The oil company hoped that, like the Gulf of Mexico to the north-east, the southern regions of the Caribbean Sea would yield some good exploration sites.

Jennifer knew that as a diver and a geologist, her father held strong views about the environment. It was only after the oil company promised to keep its impact on the local marine environment to a minimum that he agreed to work for them.

As she sat on the warm, sandy beach, watching the sunset and feasting on freshly caught seafood, Jennifer was glad that he had.

Jennifer and Peter finished their evening meal. They covered up the cooking pit with sand again, packed away the old newspapers and headed along the beach. Soon, they came to the traditional wooden chattel house they rented.

"Are you diving tomorrow, Dad?" asked Jennifer.

"Boat leaves the wharf at 8.00 am sharp," he nodded. "Plenty of time to make sure you're logged onto the distance learning website before I go," he added with a wink.

Jennifer sighed. Even being on a remote island, there were some things, like school, she just couldn't escape.

2 A Jagged Reef

The anchor of the *Blue Sunrise*, the exploration vessel that Peter was aboard, plunged into the deep blue sea. St Isabella was barely a speck on the horizon.

Peter checked his GPS and wrote down their position. With no landmarks to use as a guide, anyone mapping the seabed had to know exactly where they were.

A month before, the oil company had done an aerial survey of the area. They used complex magnetic equipment to measure changes in the earth's crust under the sea.

"This is a good area," Pete's boss, Dan O'Hara, had told him. "We old oil workers can just feel it in our bones!"

Now, as he prepared to dive with sensitive seismic detectors to place on the sea floor, he felt a sense of excitement too. As an environmentalist, he had

conflicting feelings about oil companies – but, as a geologist, he loved the idea of charting a part of Earth that no one had ever mapped before.

"Ready to go?" called Miguel, the captain of the *Blue Sunrise*. Peter smeared the inside of his mask with spit – an old diver's trick to stop a mask from steaming up – and nodded to Miguel. He checked his gear one last time and wriggled his mask firmly over his eyes and nose. Then he rolled gently backwards off the *Blue Sunrise*'s deck.

With a plume of tiny bubbles, he was in a different world. The sea seemed empty from the surface, save for a few schools of flying fish, arching their way through the air. But, below the waves, the water was teeming with colourful life. Even though he'd been diving for ten years, Peter could never shake off the delight of feeling like he was swimming in a vast tropical aquarium.

"Work to do," he reminded himself. With a kick of his flippers, he swam deeper and deeper, towards the sea floor.

Between Cuba and Jamaica to the north, trenches in the Caribbean Sea were well over 7 000 metres deep. But here, closer to the coast, the sea was shallow – only 40 metres deep. That meant the sea floor was within reach of an experienced diver like Peter.

As he descended, Peter checked his watch and his depth gauge. To return to the surface safely, he had to allow time for his body to adjust to the changes in water pressure. That meant a calm, slow descent – and a carefully timed ascent, with safety stops along the way. Shooting to the surface would mean the gases in his blood could form deadly bubbles – the dreaded "bends".

"The slower you come up, the safer you'll be," his dive teacher had told him years before. It was a piece of advice Peter took seriously. With a daughter to look after, Peter wanted to be as safe as possible.

Peter swam deeper and deeper. The colours of the sea slowly vanished until, by the time the sea floor was in sight, everything was a blue-green colour. He swam to within a metre of the sea floor and looked around. He needed to place the seismic sensors he had carried in a large triangle.

"Might as well start here," Peter thought. With a kick of his flippers, he came within reach of the sea floor and firmly planted one of the sensors.

Next, he checked the compass on his wrist and headed south-west. Keeping a count of the kicks of his flippers, Peter slowed to a halt when he reached 50. He curled down and planted another sensor.

He set off to the north-east but, instead of swimming in a straight line, he found he had to detour around a jagged coral reef that rose from the sea floor. In this part of the Caribbean Sea, a reef wasn't unusual, but this one seemed oddly narrow. Peter swam around it, adjusted his direction, and added ten kicks to his count. He planted his sensor and checked his watch. He'd been at 40 metres for 15 minutes. If he stayed any longer, he risked running out of air during his ascent.

Peter did a quick check in his mind. Swim up to 20 metres depth and wait for two minutes.

Head to 14 metres, wait for one minute. Swim up to seven metres, wait for one minute. Swim up to five metres, wait for two to five minutes. Then, rise as slowly as he could to the surface.

"Time to go," he thought. With a quick kick, he started his ascent.

Ten minutes later, Peter surfaced. He turned over onto his back and kicked towards the *Blue Sunrise*.

"All OK?" called Miguel, after Peter climbed aboard.

Peter gave the "thumbs up" sign and pulled his mask off. "Bit of a reef in the midst of the area, but the sensors are all in place."

Miguel smiled. The other people on board prepared to get the seismic survey underway. The computers they carried on board would gather the data and analyse it.

But for Peter, it was time to head below deck and pour himself a well-earned cup of hot coffee.

3 An Underwater Mystery

Peter sat at the kitchen table in the old chattel house, poring over the data that had been printed out from the morning's survey.

He'd cleaned his diving gear of salt water and hung his wetsuit on the door to dry. Jennifer sat on the other side of the table, working on the lessons she'd printed out from the distance learning website.

Outside, the palm trees rustled in the gentle evening breeze. The earliest of the crickets practised their high-pitched dusk chorus.

"That's unusual," remarked Peter, as he studied the information in front of him. The data that the *Blue Sunrise* had collected about the rocks under the sea floor was much as he'd expected – layer upon layer of soft rock, with some good drilling sites. But in the middle of the triangle, there were some odd patterns.

"That reef site is not displaying the characteristics you'd expect of a coral reef that's grown up over a solid rock base," mused Peter.

Jennifer looked up from her homework. The contour map that had been printed from one of the *Blue Sunrise*'s computers looked to her like a visual puzzle.

"Let me have a look, Dad," she said. Peter frowned.

"I've finished my work, Dad," she pleaded. "Well, most of it."

Peter smiled and slid over the contour map. He tapped the reef area with a pencil. "Here's our mystery spot," he said. "If it were solid rock underneath, we'd expect it to be a dark colour. But, as you can see, it's light – much lighter even than the sand and mud surrounding it."

Jennifer turned her head to one side and looked at the map. The long, tapering pattern in the midst of the survey area looked familiar – but what was it?

"It's bullet shaped," she said. "Like a crayon or a thick pencil stub."

Peter nodded. It reminded him of something as well, but he couldn't quite place it.

Suddenly, Jennifer sat up straight, a triumphant look across her face. "It's a ship," she declared confidently. "Look at the shape. A long, wide ship."

Peter seized the map and stared at it intently. Of course! Every day he was used to seeing the bottom of a boat – looking up, from underneath. He just hadn't expected to see this shape lying across the sea floor, 40 metres underwater.

"I think you're right, Jennifer," he said, folding his arms. He whistled. "That's why it appears as a light shade. It isn't as dense as a rock. It's hollow!"

"You've discovered a shipwreck, Dad," said Jennifer.

"A very old shipwreck," added Peter. "It would have taken centuries for that much coral to cover it and disguise it so well." He looked at Jennifer and nodded at her laptop. "If you've almost finished your work, do you mind if I borrow your laptop for a few minutes?"

Jennifer was only too glad to hand over the computer. "Help yourself, Dad," she grinned.

Peter sat back in surprise. When he'd keyed in the coordinates of the seas around St Isabella, he'd been expecting one or two results at best. But there were at least 20 ships that had been lost at sea in the area around St Isabella. Almost all of them were from the 1600s, when the Spanish conquistadors had shipped huge amounts of gold and treasure home from the newly discovered lands in the Americas. Few of the lost ships had been found. No one even knew their precise whereabouts.

“Were they sunk by pirates?” asked Jennifer excitedly.

Peter looked at the dates of the shipwrecks. Almost all of them were between June and November: hurricane season in the Caribbean.

“Probably not,” he replied. “Most likely, our mystery ship was caught in one of the storms that sweep in from the east. The sea is shallow out there. Maybe it was heading for shelter when it was hit by the storm.”

“So it might still have its treasure?” asked Jennifer.

“It might,” shrugged her father. “It might also still have other historical artefacts. We need to go back down and check it out.”

“You sure you want to go back where we were yesterday?” asked Miguel the next morning. The crew of the *Blue Sunrise* were sitting on the wharf. “We’ve got a lot of sea floor to map out there,” he said, waving his arm. “And the company wants us to get it all done by the end of the week.”

"I know," nodded Peter. "But that's a good site for drilling. We can't let it proceed if there's a wreck down there. If there is, it becomes a protected archaeological site."

Miguel frowned. "The company's not going to like that," he said, squinting in the sun. "Not after they've paid millions of dollars for their exploration licence."

Peter stood firm. "Well, let's go back and confirm whether or not it is a wreck. If it's just an odd reef, then there's no problem. Let's find out for sure."

"OK," said Miguel reluctantly. He waved at the rest of the crew and shouted something in the local Spanish dialect. Everyone headed for the gangway to the *Blue Sunrise*. Within a few minutes, the ropes holding the *Blue Sunrise* to the wharf were thrown off, and the boat made its way out to sea.

Peter rolled backwards off the deck. With a kick of his flippers, he swam towards the spot where he knew he'd find the reef. He carried a small netting bag full of tools – hammers, chisels, and a strong iron lever that could be used to prise rocks – or timbers – apart.

Because of the tools, he was heavier than usual. The descent to the sea floor was much quicker than yesterday. The pressure changes going down wouldn't cause a problem – but Peter made a mental note to take extra care going up.

"There!" he thought to himself, as he saw the strands of coral and kelp looming up from the sea floor. He kicked towards the reef. Peter knew that the growth of coral and kelp would be at its thickest on the top of the reef, so he headed for the sea floor, where he hoped the edge of the shipwreck – if it was a shipwreck – would have less growth on it.

Pulling a hammer and chisel out of the bag, he started work. As he chipped and pried the coral away, the water became cloudy, but he pressed on. Suddenly, with a sturdy hit, he almost lost grip of his tools. The chisel went right through the coral. Peter waited for the water to clear.

As the current slowly drew the cloudy water away, Peter saw the edges of the hole he'd made were splintered and rough. This was not rock. This was timber.

Peter looked anxiously at his watch. In his excitement, he'd lost track of time. Now, because he'd spent longer than he'd intended working around the edge of the wreck, he had to add valuable minutes onto his ascent time. He knew he'd make it back without having to risk a dangerous quick ascent. Still, he was cutting it fine.

4 A Race to the Wreck

Dan O'Hara was irritated. As soon as the *Blue Sunrise* had made it back to the wharf, Peter and Miguel had dialled the oil company's office in Venezuela.

"Has anybody else been told about this?" came Dan's crackly voice. The phone in the chattel house was on speaker, so both Peter and Miguel could listen.

"No," replied Peter. "I was going to call the island's governor as soon as we finished this call."

"Don't do that until I've had a chance to talk with the board," said Dan. His voice sounded as if he'd had a change of heart. "I think we all need more information before we call the government," he added calmly.

Peter looked at Miguel. He shrugged.

"Do you have any idea of what the wreck actually is?" asked Dan.

"No," said Peter. "I didn't have time to actually go inside or to see if there was anything in the interior that could identify the vessel."

"So you brought nothing up to the surface," said Dan.

"No," confirmed Peter.

"Good," came Dan's voice. "We shouldn't disturb an archaeological site anyway. It would be irresponsible to do that."

Peter nodded. He was glad that he worked for a company that behaved as it should.

"Peter, there'll be no more diving tomorrow. I'll call you at this number in the morning. Miguel, I'll talk to you later. OK?"

Both men acknowledged their boss and the phone line went dead.

"I'll come down to the *Blue Sunrise* in the morning after I've spoken to Dan," said Peter, as Miguel got up to leave. "It looks like everything's on hold until then."

"Sure thing," nodded Miguel. He waved to Jennifer, who was reading some books on the couch, and headed out the door.

"Dad, look at this," called Jennifer. "The *Nuestra Señora de Atocha* was a Spanish ship that sunk in 1622. When it was found in 1985, divers recovered gold and silver worth hundreds of millions of dollars."

Peter nodded.

"And this one. The *Nuestra Señora de la Concepcion* hit a reef after being badly damaged in a hurricane in 1659. Her cargo: 100 tons of silver and gold coin and bullion!"

"There's more gold and silver around here than anywhere else on earth," agreed Peter. "It's just that most of it is underwater." He smiled at Jennifer.

"Now, I'm pretty sure you aren't suddenly doing an assignment on Spanish shipwrecks," he said. "I think you'd better get back to your real schoolwork."

Jennifer pulled a face, but did as she was told. She knew there'd be plenty of opportunity to go back to the books once her dad returned to the kitchen table to pore over his maps and figures.

The next morning, Peter waited for the call from Dan O'Hara. He filled in his spare time by trying to find the details of possible candidates for the mystery shipwreck. From the size of the reef that covered the timber skeleton, he estimated the sunken ship was about 50 metres long. That would make it a large galleon. Out of the 20 vessels listed as lost in the seas around St Isabella, only one was a galleon: the *Nuestra Señora de San Antero*, or *Our Lady of San Antero*. Peter typed "San Antero" in the search box of an Internet map provider. Within seconds, it showed a small seaside town on the coast of modern-day Colombia. If the galleon had hugged the coastline on its voyage, it might well have found itself heading for shelter off St Isabella almost 400 years ago.

"Dad," called Jennifer. "I thought you said there'd be no diving today."

"There won't be," replied Peter. "I'm waiting for Dan O'Hara's call before we go."

"Well, where's the *Blue Sunrise* heading?" asked his daughter. She pointed out the window. There, in the distance, the exploration boat could be seen chugging its way out of the harbour.

"What?" said Peter, frowning. Suddenly the phone rang. Peter picked it up.

"We've decided you're to come to Caracas right away," came Dan O'Hara's voice. "The board wants to talk to you about this, er ... development.

We've booked a small plane to fly you off St Isabella in an hour's time. Be at the airfield in 30 minutes."

Caracas. The capital of Venezuela, hundreds of kilometres to the south.

"Hang on," said Peter. "What about the *Blue Sunrise*? What's Miguel doing?"

There was a moment of silence. "Miguel's doing something else. Don't worry about him. We need you in Caracas."

Dan O'Hara hung up. Peter frowned.

"What's up, Dad," said Jennifer.

"I don't know," replied Peter slowly. "But I'm going to find out." He quickly scribbled a handwritten note on the back of his contour map of the area around the wreck and gave it to Jennifer.

"If I'm not back by early afternoon, run down to the police base and give this to the commander."

"Dad?" said Jennifer, looking worried. "Where are you going?"

Peter pointed to the expanse of the Caribbean Sea stretching from edge to edge of the living room window. "Not to Caracas," he said determinedly. "I'm going out there."

He strode over to where his dive gear lay, slung a spare single air bottle over his shoulder, and headed towards the wharf at a run.

As well as the *Blue Sunrise*, the wharf was home to a small flotilla of fishing boats. Most had headed out to sea before dawn, but one was tied up to the wharf. Peter ran onboard. After a quick talk with the captain, he pulled out a wad of notes from his wallet. The captain smiled and unlooped a heavy rope from the wharf. Then he squeezed past the lobster pots and nets and into the bridge. A few seconds later, the engine puttered into life.

The fishing boat didn't have GPS. But that didn't matter. Peter knew that they just needed to find the *Blue Sunrise*. If he was correct, the exploration boat would be anchored right above the wreck of the *Nuestra Señora de San Antero*.

As the fishing boat chugged its way towards the horizon, Peter checked his diving gear. The air bottle was three-quarters full. He wished there was more oxygen but, as he hadn't filled his other bottle, he'd had to grab a spare.

The captain of the fishing boat called out and pointed over the bow of the boat. Peter saw a white speck.

"Take us to about 100 metres off their starboard," he shouted. The captain nodded. A quarter of an hour later, he cut the engines. The fishing boat drifted to a halt.

Peter knew that the crew of the *Blue Sunrise* would have seen them while they were still kilometres away. He knew he had to get into the water quickly. "Straight back to St Isabella," he ordered the captain of the fishing boat. "Remember what I told you."

A shout came from the *Blue Sunrise*, but Peter ignored it. He smeared the inside of his mask with some spit and headed for the port side. Then, he gently curved overboard and into the warm Caribbean sea.

5 Deep Trouble

Peter swam deeper and deeper. He checked the compass on his wrist, and curved around towards the *Blue Sunrise*.

As he approached the outline of the reef that marked the resting place of the *Nuestra Señora de San Antero*, he spotted something he hadn't expected. Everything was a green–blue colour this deep, but there was no mistaking the stripes on the explosives, bright yellow and red in the surface light, that ringed the wreck.

For a second, a chill ran up his spine. What if he was too late? What if they were about to set off the explosives? The force of the underwater explosion would crush him instantly. Then, to his relief, he saw a plume of bubbles rising from the coral on the other side of the reef.

As fast as he could, he swam directly over the wreck and its deadly explosives. As the reef dropped